Big Top Flop

Don't miss a single

Nancy Drew Clue Book:

Pool Party Puzzler

Last Lemonade Standing

A Star Witness

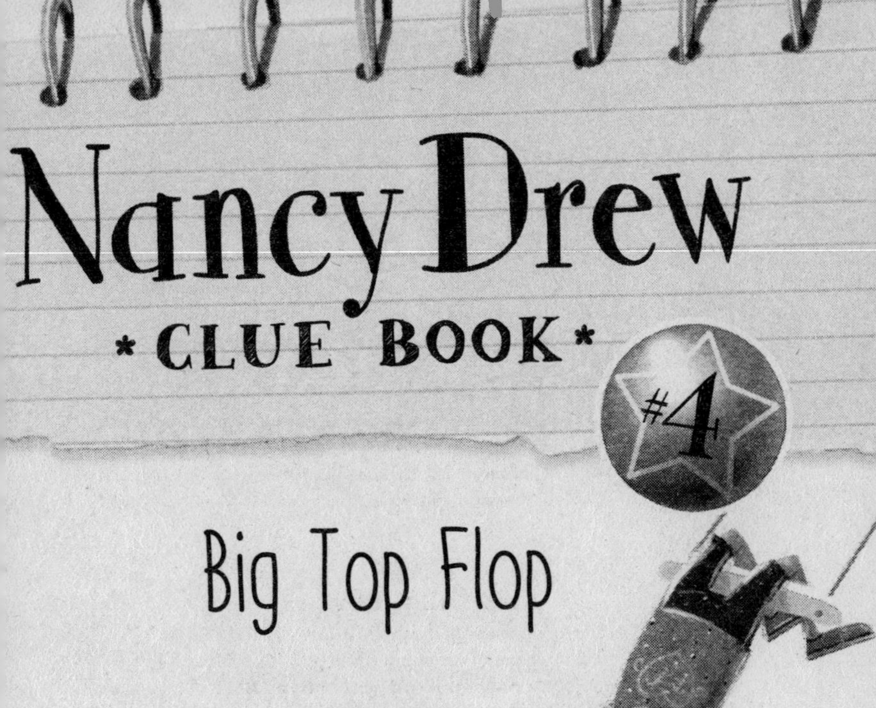

Nancy Drew

CLUE BOOK

Big Top Flop

BY CAROLYN KEENE * ILLUSTRATED BY PETER FRANCIS

Aladdin

NEW YORK LONDON TORONTO SYDNEY NEW DELHI

ALADDIN
An imprint of Simon & Schuster Children's Publishing Division
1230 Avenue of the Americas, New York, NY 10020
First Aladdin paperback edition March 2016

Also available in an Aladdin hardcover edition.

Designed by Karina Granda
The illustrations for this book were rendered digitally.
The text of this book was set in Adobe Garamond Pro.
Manufactured in the United States of America 0417 OFF
2 4 6 8 10 9 7 5 3
Library of Congress Control Number 2015937916
ISBN 978-1-4814-4000-4 (hc)
ISBN 978-1-4814-3752-3 (pbk)
ISBN 978-1-4814-3753-0 (eBook)

* CONTENTS *

Chapter

READY, SET, WHISTLE!

"The best part of spring is spring break!" George Fayne said. "And the second best part is that it begins *today*!"

"The best part of spring," Bess Marvin said, "is spring *clothes*!"

Eight-year-old Nancy Drew smiled as Bess twirled to show off her new outfit. Spring clothes and spring break were awesome. And there was one more thing about spring that she and her two best friends would totally agree on. . . .

"The best part of spring is the Bingle and Bumble Circus," Nancy declared, "which is why we're here today!"

Nancy, Bess, and George *did* agree on that. Each spring the circus came to River Heights Park. This year it came with something extra fun: a junior ringmaster contest by the big circus tent!

"Don't forget the rules!" Bess said. Her long blond ponytail bounced as she spoke. "The kid who blows a whistle the longest and loudest becomes junior ringmaster on opening day tomorrow."

"How can we forget, Bess?" George asked. "We've been practicing all week."

"I whistled so loud that my puppy, Chip, ran under my bed," Nancy said.

"That's nothing!" George said, her dark eyes wide. "I whistled so loud I broke one of my mom's catering glasses!"

"How was your whistling practice, Bess?" Nancy asked.

"I stopped when I found my baby sister sucking on my whistle," Bess said with a groan. "Gross!"

It was Friday after school, so the girls still had their backpacks. George pulled a plastic bag from hers. Inside were yellow candies shaped like lemons.

"Are those Super-Sour Suckers?" Bess asked, scrunching up her nose. "Eating those candies is like sucking lemons!"

"That's what makes them so cool!" George exclaimed. "They've got sour power!"

Nancy shook her head and said, "Sometimes I can't believe you're cousins. You two are as different as—"

"Sweet and sour?" George cut in. She was about to pop a candy into her mouth when—

"Excuse me," a boy said, "but where can a future junior ringmaster find cotton candy around here?"

Nancy, Bess, and George turned. Standing behind them was Miles Ling from the other third-grade class at school. Everyone knew that Miles wanted to be a ringmaster when he grew up. He even owned a ringmaster suit and tall black hat, which he wore today!

"You want to eat cotton candy before the contest?" Bess asked. "Won't it make your mouth too dry to whistle?"

"I don't want to *eat* the cotton candy," Miles said. "I want to stuff my ears with it!"

Nancy, Bess, and George stared at Miles.

"Stuff your ears with it?" Nancy asked slowly.

"That's how loud I whistle," Miles explained. "And when I whistle in the contest, you'll need some too!"

Nancy and her friends traded eye rolls. Miles may have been a good whistler, but he was also a very good bragger!

"We don't have any cotton candy," George said. "But you can have a Super-Sour Sucker."

George held out the bag. When Miles looked down at it his eyes popped wide open.

"N-no, thanks. . . . I've got to go," Miles

blurted. He then turned quickly and disappeared in the crowd.

"Do you think Miles was serious about stuffing cotton candy in his ears?" Bess asked.

"No," George said. "But he is serious about winning the Junior Ringmaster Contest."

"Well, so are we!" Nancy said, smiling. "In fact, let's make a deal. If one of us wins, we'll bring the other two to the circus on opening night."

"Sure, we will, Nancy," Bess agreed. "After all, we're a team even when we're not solving mysteries!"

Nancy and her friends loved solving mysteries more than anything. They even had their own detective club called the Clue Crew. Nancy owned a notebook where she wrote down all her clues and suspects. She called it her Clue Book, and she carried it wherever she went.

The girls turned to gaze at the big white circus tent with red stripes. Past the tent were rows of trailers.

"That's probably where the circus people and

animals stay," George pointed out. "Who are your favorites?"

Nancy smiled as she remembered the circus from last spring. "Oodles of Poodles are the best!" she said.

"I like Shirley the Seesaw Llama!" Bess said excitedly. "No one rides a seesaw like Shirley!"

"The Flying Fabuloso Family rocks!" George said. "Especially the trapeze twins, Fifi and Felix!"

"Fifi and Felix?" Bess said with a frown. "Those twins are trouble times two!"

"When they aren't on the trapeze," Nancy said, "they're playing tricks on other circus people!"

"Last year Fifi and Felix put some trick soap in Ringmaster Rex's trailer," Bess added. "His face was blue throughout the whole show!"

George shrugged and said, "The circus is all about tricks, right?"

Nancy was about to answer when the crowd began to cheer. She turned toward the tent just as Ringmaster Rex stepped out, waving his tall black hat!

"There he is!" Nancy said.

"And his face isn't blue!" Bess said with relief.

Mayor Strong and more circus people filed out of the tent. Fifi and Felix Fabuloso marched behind their parents.

"Will all kids please form a single line?" Mayor Strong asked. "Lulu the Clown is about to come around with a bag full of whistles."

The line formed lickety-split. The girls landed in the back with Miles right behind them.

"The best always goes last!" Miles bragged. "And that would be me!"

George groaned under her breath. "No wonder Miles is a good whistler," she whispered. "He's a total windbag!"

Lulu the Clown, wearing a gray wig, baggy dress, and striped stockings, walked down the line with her bag of whistles. One by one the kids reached inside and pulled out a whistle until—

"Eeeeeeeek!" a voice cried.

What happened? Nancy, Bess, and George stepped out of the line to see. A girl with curly blond hair had just pulled a giant squirmy spider from Lulu the Clown's bag. But when she threw it on the ground—it bounced!

"It's made out of rubber," the girl said, staring at the spider. "But it's still icky."

Mayor Strong raised an eyebrow and said, "Are you clowning around with these kids, Lulu?"

"I didn't put that spider in the bag," Lulu insisted. She pointed to Fifi and Felix snicker-

ing to each other. "It's those Fabuloso Twins and their tricks!"

Nancy frowned. No surprise there!

"I thought the circus was supposed to be *inside* the tent!" Ringmaster Rex sighed. "Let's get on with the contest, shall we?"

Nancy, Bess, and George each pulled a whistle from Lulu's bag. So did Miles. When everyone had a whistle—

"Let the contest begin!" Ringmaster Rex boomed.

Nancy and her friends waited while other kids blew their whistles long and loud near the front of the tent. Finally it was their turns!

Nancy gave her whistle a long tweet but stopped when her nose began to tickle. Bess blew her whistle until she got the giggles. Then came George's turn and . . .

TWEEEEEEEEEEEEEEEEEEEEEEE!

Everyone clapped their hands over their ears. George's whistle was so loud that even the horses in the circus tent whinnied!

George finally stopped to catch her breath. The crowd began to cheer. George was a whistling superstar!

"Way to go!" Nancy cried as George hurried back.

"You mean 'way to blow'!" George joked.

"Not bad," Miles told the girls as he walked to the front of the tent with his whistle. "Now prepare to be *blown* away."

"Don't worry, George," Bess said, handing her the bag of Super-Sour Suckers. George had asked Bess to hold them while she whistled. "You're the whistling champ so far!"

The girls looked on as Miles held his whistle between his thumb and pointer fingers. After clearing his throat he shouted, "Ladies and gentlemen and children of all ages! Introducing the junior ringmaster with the biggest, loudest whistle in the West . . . the East . . . the—"

"We don't have all day, kid," Ringmaster Rex said.

Miles stuck the whistle in his mouth. His chest

puffed out, then, *TWEEEEEEEEEEEEEEEEE!*

Nancy gulped. Miles really was an awesome whistler. But would he whistle longer and harder than George?

Miles's eyes darted around as he whistled. But when his eyes landed on George they popped wide open. Suddenly—*CLUNK*—the whistle dropped out of Miles's mouth. Miles's lips began to pucker, then his whole face!

The crowd laughed at Miles's funny faces. Nancy had a feeling it wasn't a joke. Especially when Miles stopped puckering and pointed angrily at George.

"It's all her fault!" Miles shouted. "She did it on purpose!"

Nancy turned to George, a Super-Sour Sucker lodged in her cheek.

Did *what*?

Chapter 2

NO SMILES FOR MILES

The crowd was still laughing as Miles stormed over to George. His hand trembled as he pointed to the bag of Super-Sour Suckers in George's hand.

"Just looking at those candies makes me pucker!" Miles complained. "That's why you ate them in front of me!"

"What?" Nancy said with disbelief.

"So I would lose the contest!" Miles said.

"How should I know Super-Sour Suckers

make you pucker?" George asked. "We're not even in the same class."

"Don't even say s-s-super-s-s-sour," Miles stammered, his face twitching again. Suddenly—

"Attention boys and girls!" Ringmaster Rex boomed. "The Bingle and Bumble Circus agrees that the winner of the Junior Ringmaster Contest is—"

"Georgia Fayne!" Mayor Strong chimed in.

"Yaaaaaay!!!" Nancy and Bess cheered.

"Did he have to say Georgia?" George said, cringing at her real name.

"And since Miles Ling made such funny faces," Mayor Strong went on. "The circus wants to make him junior clown tomorrow on opening day!"

Nancy smiled at Miles. She expected him to be smiling too. Instead his face glowed with rage.

"Clown?" Miles cried. "I didn't go to circus camp for three whole summers to be called clown!"

"Harsh," Lulu the Clown muttered.

Miles shot George one last glare before stomping off through the crowd.

George shook her head and said, "Remind me never to go trick-or-treating with Miles on Halloween. Did you ever see such a candy meltdown?"

"Don't worry, George," Bess said. "You didn't do anything wrong."

"You're going to be junior ringmaster tomorrow," Nancy added excitedly. "And we're going to the Bingle and Bumble Circus!"

The next day, Saturday, couldn't come fast enough for Nancy, Bess, and George. At one o'clock sharp the girls were driven straight to the park by Hannah Gruen.

Hannah was the Drews' housekeeper, but she was more like a mother to Nancy. She gave the best hugs, baked the best oatmeal cookies, and laughed at Nancy's riddles even if she had heard them dozens of times before.

As they walked onto the circus grounds,

Nancy gasped, "Look at all those people!"

"They're here to see the circus!" Bess said.

"And me!" George added a bit nervously.

It was too early for the show, but it was not too early to watch jugglers, acrobats, and clowns practicing right outside the tent.

Hannah was busy watching a man juggle plates when—*WOOF!* A snowy white poodle wearing a big collar charged toward the girls. Running after it was a boy of about nine years old.

"Gotcha!" the boy said, grabbing the dog.

Nancy smiled at the dog. "Omigosh—is that one of the Oodles of Poodles?" she asked.

The boy nodded, then introduced himself. "My name is Alberto," he said. "I'm helping my parents train the poodles during my spring break."

"That must be so cool," George said.

"Most of the time it is," Alberto said. "But Celeste here is hard to train. Today she refuses to wear her costume!"

Celeste gave a little yap before jumping out of Alberto's arms.

"See what I mean?" Alberto groaned before running after Celeste.

"I don't blame Celeste for not liking her costume," Bess said. "That collar looked itchy!"

Hannah walked over with a woman at her side. The woman was dressed in a Bingle and Bumble T-shirt and khaki pants.

"Girls, meet Peggy Bingle!" Hannah said excitedly. "Her great-great-grandfather started the Bingle and Bumble Circus almost a hundred years ago!"

"I guess you can say I have sawdust in my blood," Peggy said with a smile.

"That's got to hurt," George said.

"It's a figure of speech, dear," Peggy said. "How would you like a tour of the circus grounds before I show our junior ringmaster her very own trailer?"

"That would be George!" Bess said proudly.

Hannah was invited to have coffee in the circus performers' lounge while Nancy and her friends followed Peggy. They walked past the tent to what Peggy called the "Back Yard." She explained how the circus performers lived in trailers so they could travel from town to town. Some trailers were painted bright colors.

There were also a few smaller tents, like a polka-dotted tent called "Clown Alley," plus a big open tent that served food to the staff and performers. The girls were surprised to see everyone eating chicken, salad, and potatoes.

"I thought circus people only ate cotton candy and peanuts!" Bess admitted.

Peggy let the girls peek inside the wardrobe trailer, where bright sparkly costumes hung everywhere. A seamstress named Pearl sat at a sewing machine mending last-minute rips and tears.

"What's that loud rumbling noise?" Nancy asked as they walked away from the trailer.

"You mean that *growl*?" Peggy asked. The girls gasped as she pointed to cages and dens housing two tigers, horses—even a baby elephant!

"Do all the circus animals live here?" Nancy asked.

"All but Oodles of Poodles and Shirley the Seesaw Llama," Peggy explained. "They have trailers of their own."

"That's because Shirley's a star!" Bess said.

"Everybody is a star at Bingle and Bumble Circus!" Peggy said. She smiled at George. "Now let's show our junior ringmaster *her* trailer!"

Peggy led the girls to a shiny silver trailer. She opened the door and the girls filed inside.

The first thing Nancy saw was a ringmaster suit hanging from a rack. It had black pants and a red jacket with gold buttons. A shelf on top of the rack held a tall black hat just like Ringmaster Rex's!

"Is that mine?" George asked.

Peggy nodded and said, "Why don't you change into your suit right away? I'll knock on your door at show time."

Peggy left the trailer, and George ran straight to her costume. She was about to grab the jacket when—

"Wait!" Bess said. She pointed to a small sink in the corner. "Don't touch that beautiful costume until your *hands* are as clean as a whistle!"

"Since when are whistles clean?" George joked. "They're full of spit."

George did wash her hands, though. She then slipped on her ringmaster suit and hat.

"Ta-daaa!" George declared.

"Awesome!" Nancy said. "But something is missing."

"What?" George asked.

Nancy looked around the trailer until she spotted a long, silver object on the vanity table.

"That!" Nancy said, pointing to the table. "There's your whistle, Ringmaster George!"

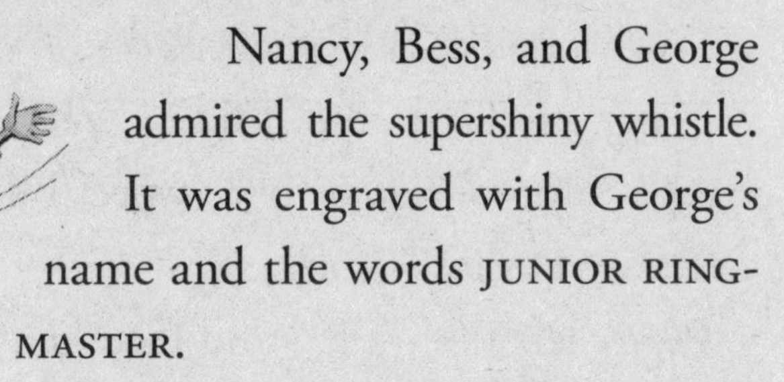

Nancy, Bess, and George admired the supershiny whistle. It was engraved with George's name and the words JUNIOR RINGMASTER.

"They wrote George," George said with relief. "Not Georgia!"

"And this one can't be full of spit," Bess said with a smile. "It's brand-new!"

"Try it out, George," Nancy said excitedly.

George was about to give it a tweet when—*whoosh*—something slid under the door. It was a note written with green ink. Nancy picked it up and read it out loud: "'You're all invited to a cotton-candy party in the big circus tent. Come over right now!'"

"Cotton candy—yum!" Bess cheered.

"But Peggy wanted us to wait here," Nancy said.

"Maybe the note came from Peggy," George said, putting the whistle back on the table. "We should go to the party."

The girls left the tent, making sure to close

the door behind them. They rushed to the big tent and peered through the canvas opening. There was no party inside—only a few grown-up Fabulosos practicing a trapeze act. Their purple glittery leotards sparkled as they swung high above.

"No cotton-candy party in there," George said.

"Phooey," Bess said, disappointed.

Nancy didn't get it. "Then who sent that note?" she wondered out loud. Then—

"There you are!" Peggy called, rushing over. "The guests are about to enter the tent. George, we're almost ready for you."

"Okay!" George said. "I just have to go back to my trailer for my whistle."

"She'll be back in a flash, Ms. Bingle," Nancy promised. She, Bess, and George rushed back to the trailer.

Bess shivered as they walked inside. "Why is it so cold in here all of a sudden?" she said.

"Who cares?" George said, grabbing the

ringmaster whistle from the vanity table. "It's show time!"

The girls raced back to the big tent. George was whisked away by one of the show directors. An usher led Nancy and Bess inside the tent. Hannah was waiting in their special grandstand seats, right next to the circus ring!

"Watch out for swinging horse tails!" Hannah teased.

Nancy was so excited she could hardly breathe—especially when the lights flashed off and a spotlight began to swirl!

"Ladies, gentlemen, and children of all ages!" a man's voice boomed over the loudspeaker. "Please welcome Ringmaster Rex and our special guest, Junior Ringmaster George Fayne!"

"Yaaaaaay!" Nancy and Bess cheered louder than anyone as Ringmaster Rex and George entered the ring. When the cheering died down Rex and George stood in the spotlight.

"George?" Rex asked in a deep voice. "Do you have your whistle ready?"

"Sure do, Ringmaster Rex!" George replied.

"Then give a whistle, and let the circus begin!" Rex shouted.

Nancy and Bess squeezed hands as George put the whistle between her lips. Her chest puffed out and both shoulders rose. She leaned forward as she began to blow. There was just one problem: No sound came out!

"Where's the whistle?" Bess whispered.

"I don't know!" Nancy whispered back.

George's face seemed to redden as she blew even harder. Her arm flapped up and down as she kept trying to whistle. But no matter how hard George seemed to blow, there was no sound!

"Oh no!" Nancy groaned as she watched George. "Something is wrong!"

Chapter

FLEE-RING CIRCUS

"I can do it! Let me try again!" George cried as Peggy gently dragged her out of the ring. But before George could stick the whistle back in her mouth . . .

TWEEEEEEEEEEEEEEEEEEE!!! Ringmaster Rex blew his own whistle and shouted, "Let the circus begin!"

George was led away, just as a parade of circus performers marched into the ring. Any other time Nancy and Bess would have been happy to see them, but not this time.

"Hannah, I want to leave and find George," Nancy said.

"Me too," Bess agreed.

"But you girls will miss Oodles of Poodles," Hannah said. "And Shirley the Seesaw Llama."

Nancy could see her favorite poodles and Shirley in the parade. Also marching were Fifi and Felix Fabuloso in their own sparkly purple leotards.

"Shirley and the poodles aren't our best friends, Hannah," Nancy said. "George is."

"I'll save your seats," Hannah said with a smile. "But be back here in a half hour. No later."

Nancy glanced at her watch and promised to be back on time. As the horses pranced into the middle of the ring she and Bess stood up and walked out of the tent.

"There she is!" Bess cried.

Nancy looked to see where Bess was pointing. George was racing to her trailer. "George, wait!" she called.

"They gave me a broken whistle!" George shouted back as she kept running. "How could they do that to me?"

Once inside the trailer George slammed the whistle on the vanity table. Nancy tilted her head as she looked it over. Something about it was different.

"The whistle isn't as shiny as it was before," Nancy said.

"Maybe George smudged it with her fingerprints," Bess said while George slipped out of her ringmaster suit.

But when Nancy picked it up, she noticed something else. "George's name is gone!" she gasped. "So are the words 'junior ringmaster'!"

"You mean it's a different whistle?" Bess asked.

"Can't be," George said, still frowning. "It's broken. That's all."

Nancy shook her head and said, "I think the real ringmaster whistle was *switched* with a broken whistle."

George wrinkled her nose as she stared at

Nancy. "When did that happen?" she asked.

"Maybe when we left to look for the party," Nancy said. "Whoever slipped us the fake invitation probably wanted us to leave the trailer so they could do the switcheroo."

"But this is the circus—everybody is happy and nice!" Bess cried. "Who would do something like that?"

"I don't know, Bess," Nancy admitted. "But the Clue Crew can try to find out."

Nancy put the whistle back on the table. She reached into the pocket of her jacket and pulled out her Clue Book.

"You really do bring your Clue Book everywhere," George said, cracking a small smile. "Even to the circus!"

"And I'm glad I did!" Nancy said as she opened her book. A pen was tucked inside. She used it to write the words, "Who Switched Whistles?" Under that she wrote "Clues."

"The first clue was the invitation," Nancy said as she wrote, "written with green ink."

"There's another clue!" George said, pointing to patches of sandy dust on the floor. "Sawdust!"

"The circus ring is filled with sawdust," Bess said. "You must have gotten some on your shoes inside the tent."

"Ringmaster Rex and I walked in on a clear plastic runner," George said. She pointed down at her clean shoes. "My shoes never touched sawdust!"

"Then someone from the circus ring tracked sawdust in here," Nancy decided. "Maybe a circus performer!"

"Or a sourpuss!" Bess said angrily.

Sour? The word gave Nancy another idea!

"Miles Ling was mad at George for sucking sour candies while he was trying to whistle in the contest," Nancy said.

"And Miles was asked to be a junior clown!" Bess added. "Which means he's probably here today!"

"We have no proof that a clown was in this trailer," George said. "Like footprints from giant shoes."

"No," Bess said with a smile, "but we do have *that*!"

Bess pointed under the vanity table. Nancy looked under the table and saw something red, small, and round. She picked it up, and it squeaked!

"It's a red rubber clown nose!" Nancy exclaimed.

"And it's small enough to belong to a kid!" George pointed out. "A kid like Miles."

"Does that mean I found a clue?" Bess asked.

"Yes!" Nancy said. "And now we're going to find our first suspect—Miles Ling!

Chapter

SAY SQUEEZE!

Nancy looked at her watch as the girls left the trailer. She remembered her promise to Hannah to be back at the tent in a half hour.

"We have ten minutes to find and question Miles," Nancy told her friends. "So we have to work fast."

"Miles could be anywhere here at the circus," Bess said. "Where do we look first?"

The girls spotted a jumble of arrow-shaped

signs pointing in all directions. Nancy read the signs out loud: "'Food Carts' . . . 'Blacksmith Shop' . . . 'Junior Clown Alley'—"

"That's it!" George said. "That must be where the Junior Clowns hang out."

The arrow-shaped sign pointed to a small white tent with colorful polka dots. The Clue Crew raced over to it. They peeked through the opening and looked around.

"No clowns in there," George said.

"No anybody," Bess added.

"Let's go in," Nancy suggested. "Maybe we can find clues that Miles was here."

The girls slipped inside the tent. It was filled with colorful clown props like giant baseball bats, tiny tricycles, and squirting soda bottles. A long table with mirrors held pots of gooey clown makeup and crazy wigs!

"Cool!" George said, pulling a rainbow-colored wig over her curly dark hair. "I've always wanted one of these!"

"And I've always wanted a pair of these!" Bess said, slipping into a pair of gigantic clown shoes.

George plopped a funny hat over Nancy's reddish blond hair. "Try this on for size, Nancy!" she said.

"There's no time to clown around, you guys!" Nancy said. "We have to look for clues that Miles was in here!"

Still wearing the clown gear, the Clue Crew searched for traces of Miles. But Bess found something else. . . .

"A clown car!" Bess cried out. "Let's see if we can all squeeze inside just like clowns do!"

Nancy turned. Bess was already squeezing inside a tiny car with big wheels. It was bright red and yellow.

"Come on, Nancy," George called as she crammed inside too. "Pile in!"

Nancy stared at the tiny clown car. She had always wondered what it was like to be inside one, so . . .

"Okay, but let's be quick," Nancy warned.

"Those Junior Clowns and Miles could be here any second!"

Squeezing inside the clown car was a tight fit for Nancy, Bess, and George—so tight that Bess wanted out!

"My foot is practically in my face!" Bess complained. "And I'm wearing giant shoes!"

"I don't like it either, Bess," Nancy said. "It's dark and stuffy in here."

"It's a plastic clown car, you guys!" George groaned. "Not a luxury stretch limo!"

Nancy was about to open the car door when she heard the sound of voices and loud thumping footsteps!

"Somebody's coming!" Nancy hissed.

"And they've got big feet!" George said quietly.

"Big feet mean clowns!" Bess whispered.

The Clue Crew sat silently inside the tiny car. They wanted to find Miles, but they didn't want the Junior Clowns to find them snooping inside their tent!

Nancy peered out the car's window. She could see about five Junior Clowns stepping inside.

"It's just our luck we had to be in the ring with Shirley the Spitting Llama!" a girl with a bright-red clown wig said.

"You mean Shirley the Seesaw Llama?" a boy asked.

"She's the spitting llama to me," the girl replied. "Clowns may rule but llamas drool!"

Nancy felt Bess tug her sleeve.

"I'm getting a cramp in my foot!" Bess whispered.

"Wiggle it!" Nancy whispered back.

The car shook slightly as Bess wiggled her foot with the giant clown shoe. Then—

HOOOOOOONNNNNNNNNKKK!!!

Nancy, Bess, and George froze. Bess's giant clown foot had pressed the car horn!

"Hey," a clown said. "There's only one way to blow the horn and that's"—the girls gasped as the clown yanked the door open—"inside!"

Nancy and her friends spilled out of the tiny car. As they stood up they were surrounded by junior clowns!

"What were you doing in our car?" the girl with the red wig demanded.

"And what are you doing with our wig, hat, and shoes?" the boy wanted to know.

The clowns wore lots of makeup, red round noses, and giant plastic flowers on their jackets. Their names were stitched onto their jackets too, but not one of them was Miles.

"We just wanted to try on some fun clown things, that's all," Nancy explained.

"We're junior clowns too," Bess blurted. "Just like you guys."

Nancy heard George groan under her breath. Nancy had a feeling Bess's answer meant trouble.

"Oh yeah?" Mandy, the red-wig clown, said. "If you're junior clowns, then show us your best tricks."

"Tricks?" Nancy repeated.

"Every clown knows tricks," Spencer, a boy clown, said. "That is . . . if you really are junior clowns."

Nancy gulped. If she did know any tricks, she couldn't think of one now!

"Just go for it," George muttered. She picked up two juggling balls, but when she tried to juggle—*clunk, clunk*—dropped them on the ground!

Nancy turned a cartwheel. Bess hopped up and down on one giant foot.

Mandy pointed to the girls and shouted,

"Wannabes! I'll bet you never went to circus camp a day in your life!"

"Let's show them *our* favorite trick!" Spencer told the other clowns. "Shall we?"

The clowns formed a circle around the girls. Nancy gulped again. Now what?

"Ready? Aim?" Mandy shouted. "Gush!"

Nancy, Bess, and George shrieked. The flowers on the clown's jackets squirted water straight at them.

"Okay!" Nancy shouted as the water kept gushing. "We'll tell you why we're really here—just stoooooopppp!!!"

Chapter

SLICK TRICK

The clowns finally stopped, but it was too late. Nancy, Bess, and George were dripping wet!

Nancy spit out a mouthful of water. "We're here to look for Miles Ling," she said. "Do any of you know him?"

While the clowns whispered to one another, Nancy studied their noses. They seemed different than the nose they found in the trailer.

"A couple of us know Miles from circus camp," a clown named Chloe said. "He used to get candy ringmaster whistles in his care packages."

"We know Miles wanted to be junior ringmaster," George said. "He became a junior clown at the whistle contest instead."

"Nuh-uh," Arlen said, shaking his head. "Something more awesome happened to Miles after the whistle contest."

"What happened?" Nancy asked.

"Miles went to Chicago with his parents," Arlen explained, "to film a commercial for Super-Sour Suckers."

"But Miles hates Super-Sour Suckers!" Bess said.

"A commercial director was at the contest," Arlen said. "He liked Miles's funny faces and asked him to pucker like that on TV."

"How do you know for sure?" Nancy asked.

"I was at the contest too," Arlen said. "I saw the whole thing!"

The Clue Crew traded looks. Was Arlen telling the truth about Miles? Or was he just clowning around?

Chloe interrupted the girls' thoughts as she

pointed to George. "Hey!" she said. "Aren't you the junior ringmaster who can't whistle?"

"My whistle couldn't whistle," George muttered.

"Bummer!" Mandy said. She held out a tall, colorful can. "Have some yummy peanut brittle to cheer up."

"I love peanut brittle!" Bess said, grabbing the can. But when she opened it three fake snakes sprang out of the can into the air!

"Very funny," Nancy told the clowns while Bess screamed.

"Sure, we're funny!" Arlen said with a grin. "We're clowns!"

The girls returned the clown gear before leaving Junior Clown Alley.

"I don't think Miles was at the circus today," Nancy said. "And that nose we found didn't belong to a junior clown, either."

"How do you know, Nancy?" Bess asked.

Nancy had the rubber nose in her jacket pocket. She pulled it out and placed it over her real nose.

"This nose is tiny," Nancy pointed out. "Even for a kid."

"There you are!" someone called.

Nancy turned to see Hannah walking toward them. She looked relieved but also a bit mad.

"I was looking all over for you," Hannah said.

"Sorry, Hannah," Nancy said. "We were busy doing something and forgot about the time."

Hannah looked the girls up and down. "You're

all soaking wet," she said. "How can you see the rest of the circus like that?"

"I think we've had enough of the circus today, Hannah." George sighed.

"And clowns," Bess added.

They were about to head for the car when George remembered something.

"I have to run back to my trailer," George said. "I left my jacket in there."

"Okay," Hannah said. "But this time—"

"We'll be right back," Nancy said. "Promise!"

Nancy, Bess, and George raced to the silver trailer. A blast of cold air hit them as they walked inside.

"No wonder it's so cold in here!" Bess said. She pointed to one of the windows in the trailer. It was half open.

Nancy stared up at the window. Did someone open it from outside?

"You guys," Nancy asked slowly, "do you think the whistle-switcher climbed in through the window?"

"The window is high," George said. "Why would someone climb through the window if the door wasn't locked?"

"So he or she wouldn't be seen going into the trailer?" Nancy wondered. She dragged a chair underneath the window and climbed up onto it.

"What are you doing, Nancy?" George asked.

"I want to see if there's a tree outside," Nancy explained. "Maybe the whistle-switcher climbed it to get through the window."

But when Nancy reached the window, she found something else. Scattered all over the windowsill was—

"Purple glitter!" Nancy gasped.

"So?" George asked.

"The Fabuloso Family was wearing purple glitter leotards!" Nancy said excitedly. "So were Fifi and Felix!"

"If anyone could climb way up there," George said, narrowing her eyes. "It's the Flying Fabulosos!"

"Fifi and Felix are always playing tricks too," Bess said.

Nancy hopped off the chair and smiled. Not only did she just discover a glittery clue, she discovered two new suspects!

"Maybe Fifi and Felix had a brand-new trick," Nancy said, clapping her hands to get rid of the purple glitter on them. "And this time it wasn't on the trapeze!"

Chapter

TWIN SPIN

"Thanks for driving us to the park today, Daddy," Nancy said the next morning. "What will you do while we work on our case?"

"I'll read the Sunday paper here in the car," Mr. Drew said as he drove. "How would you girls like to work on the puzzles in the kids section?"

Nancy shook her head as she sat between Bess and George in the backseat.

"No, thanks, Daddy," Nancy said. "The only puzzle we want to solve right now is our mystery!"

Nancy had already told her dad about the case of the switched whistles.

"Do you have any suspects?" Mr. Drew asked.

"We're pretty sure Fifi and Felix Fabuloso did the switcheroo, Mr. Drew," George said.

"The proof is in the glitter!" Bess added.

Mr. Drew was a lawyer but often thought like a detective. He smiled at the girls in the rearview mirror and said, "Just be careful not to accuse Fifi and Felix right away."

"Why not, Daddy?" Nancy asked.

"Because sometimes even your proof needs proof," Mr. Drew replied.

Before Nancy could ask what he meant, Mr. Drew pulled up to the park.

"Thanks again, Daddy!" Nancy said as she and her friends filed out. "See you after we find Fifi and Felix!"

"Where do you think the twins are?" George asked as they walked away from the car.

"Maybe in their trailer getting ready for the next show," Nancy said.

"Or their next *trick*!" Bess said with a frown.

The Clue Crew reached the circus grounds. They were about to walk past the big tent toward the trailers when—

"Excuse me, girls," someone said.

Nancy and her friends turned. A guard stood behind them. The name on her shiny silver badge read FRAN.

"Kids aren't allowed on the circus grounds until a half hour before the show," Fran said.

Nancy knew they had to look for Fifi and Felix right away.

"George was the junior ringmaster yesterday,

and she forgot something in her trailer," Nancy blurted. "Can we go there and look for it, please?"

"It's her favorite pink hair barrette!" Bess added.

"Yuck, Bess!" George cried horrified. "Since when do I ever wear pink hair barrettes?"

Nancy was about to jump in when she noticed Fran smiling at George.

"So you're the one who couldn't whistle?" Fran asked.

"That was me," George muttered.

"Tough luck, kid," Fran said. She nodded toward the trailers in the distance. "You can go to your trailer and look for that pink barrette. Just don't stay long, okay?"

Nancy thanked Fran. As the girls rushed toward the trailers, George pulled the broken whistle from her pocket.

"Even the guard thinks I'm a whistling loser!" George complained. "Why won't this dumb thing work?"

George stuck the whistle in her mouth. Puffing

her cheeks, she tried to get a sound out of it. It was no use.

"It doesn't work, George," Nancy said.

"And you look like a blowfish!" Bess giggled.

George dropped the whistle back in her pocket. As the girls walked, they could hear dogs barking in the distance.

"We know Oodles of Poodles are here today," Nancy said with a smile. "But where are Fifi and Felix?"

"There!" Bess said excitedly.

Nancy looked to see where Bess was pointing. Coming out of the snack tent and eating bananas were the twins!

"Hey!" George shouted. "Fifi and Felix!"

The twins turned around. They were wearing light jackets over their purple leotards.

"What's up?" Felix called back.

"We want to know if you switched something in George's trailer yesterday," Nancy called.

The twins traded sly grins. Then Fifi said, "Maybe we did it."

"Maybe we didn't," Felix added and snickered.

Nancy frowned. The trapeze-twirling twins were tough nuts to crack. But before she could ask more questions, Fifi gave her brother a nudge.

"Whatever you do," Fifi whispered loud enough for the girls to hear, "don't let them see what's in your pocket!"

Pockets? The Clue Crew glanced down at the pockets on Felix's jacket. Both were lumpy with stuff. But what kind of stuff?

"I'll bet my whistle is in there!" George snapped. "The good whistle you switched with a dud!"

The twins spun on their heels and shot off!

"Don't let them get away!" Nancy cried.

The Clue Crew ran after Fifi and Felix. They were about to catch up when the twins tossed their banana peels in their path. Nancy, Bess, and George froze to a stop. Banana peels were slippery!

"They ran around the tent!" George shouted.

The girls jumped over the banana peels and raced around the tent. There they found the Fabuloso twins swinging from trapezes!

"Get down right now!" Nancy called. "And show us what's in your pockets!"

"Come and get us!" Fifi shouted as the two swung higher and faster.

"If you're not afraid of heights!" Felix laughed.

"Great," Nancy whispered. "We'll never be able to search Felix's pockets all the way up there!"

"Oh yeah?" George whispered with a grin. "Watch *this*!"

Chapter

WASH AND CRY

What was George's plan? Nancy didn't have a clue as she and Bess followed George to the trapezes. But they were about to find out.

"Your swinging is awesome!" George shouted up to the twins. "But I bet you can't swing upside down!"

"Oh yeah?" Felix shouted back.

"Let's show them!" Fifi called to her brother. "On my count. Three . . . two . . . one . . . FLIP!"

In a flash the twins flipped upside down, still

hanging from their legs. As they swung back and forth—*CLATTER, CLATTER, CLUNK*—stuff from both twins' pockets spilled out all over the ground!

So that was George's plan!

"Ye-es!" Nancy cheered under her breath as they ran toward the stuff. "Let's look for the whistle!"

The girls scooped up two packs of bubblegum, a balled-up tissue that made Bess gag, a pen, and—

"A bar of soap?" Nancy said, picking it up. That was a weird thing to have in a pocket!

"But no whistle," George said sadly. "Anywhere."

Fifi and Felix were already on solid ground as they glared at the girls.

"You tricked us!" Fifi complained.

"Us?" George snorted. "If anyone knows about tricks it's you two."

"Where's George's whistle?" Nancy asked.

"What whistle?" Felix asked.

"George's ringmaster whistle that was switched

with a broken one!" Bess said. "As if you didn't know!"

"We found purple glitter on the windowsill of George's trailer," Nancy explained. "Just like the purple glitter on your leotards."

Fifi looked down at her leotard. "That's not purple," she said. "It's violet!"

"Give me a break," George muttered.

Suddenly the pen dropped out of Nancy's hands onto the ground.

"Nancy, that pen is green," Bess pointed. "Wasn't the party invitation written with green ink?"

George didn't mind getting dirty. She grabbed the pen and scribbled a squiggly line on her wrist . . . a green squiggly line!

"You wrote that party invitation to get us out of the trailer," George told the twins.

"So you could do the switcheroo!" Bess added.

"Okay, we did make a switch," Fifi said, "but it wasn't whistles."

"What was it?" Nancy demanded.

“Fifi! Felix!” a woman called.

Nancy turned to see Mrs. Fabuloso, wearing her own purple leotard.

“Come to the tent, kids,” Mrs. Fabuloso called. “Uncle Alfonso is swinging by his teeth and wants you to watch!”

“In a minute, Mom!” Fifi called. She turned to the girls and said, “We’ll take back our stuff now!”

Nancy and her friends handed Fifi and Felix everything they had picked up, including the green pen. The twins stuffed their pockets, and then they raced toward the big tent.

“They did say they switched something,” Nancy said. “But they didn’t say what.”

“It still could have been the whistles!” George said. “And what kid carries a bar of soap around with him?”

Bess wrinkled her nose and said, “Speaking of soap, can I wash my hands? I touched that gross tissue!”

“There was a sink in George’s trailer,” Nancy suggested. “Let’s see if it’s still open.”

The door to George's trailer was still unlocked. Nancy knocked three times. When no one answered she opened the door and they stepped inside.

"It's empty," George said. "I guess no one moved in after me."

"While Bess washes her hands, we can look for more clues," Nancy said.

Bess hurried to the sink and turned on the water. Nancy and George walked slowly around the trailer, looking up and down and all around.

"I'm pretty sure the twins snuck in here to switch whistles," Nancy admitted.

"Me too," George agreed. "What else is there to switch in here?"

Suddenly—

"Eeeek!!!" Bess screamed.

Nancy and George looked toward the sink. Bess was turning around slowly, horrified.

"Bess, what happened?" Nancy asked.

"My hands!" Bess cried. "They're . . . blue!"

Chapter

SEE-REX!

Nancy and George stared at Bess's hands. They were blue—bright blue!

"How did that happen?" Nancy gasped.

"The soap on the sink is white!" George said, pointing to the sink.

"Then it must be trick soap!" Bess wailed.

"I washed in here yesterday," George said. "And I don't look like a Smurf!"

Nancy was still thinking about the word

"trick." It made her think of two people: Fifi and Felix Fabuloso!

"Fifi and Felix switched Ringmaster Rex's soap once," Nancy said. "And they said they switched something here."

"So they switched soap?" George asked.

"No wonder Felix had soap in his pocket," Bess said. "That was the good soap he switched with the trick kind."

"Okay," George agreed. "But while they were

here, those twins could have switched whistles, too!"

Nancy shook her head. "If they did, then your real whistle would have been in Felix's pocket," she said. "I think the twins are clean."

"But my hands aren't!" Bess cried. "How do I get this blue stuff off?"

"Let's ask Ringmaster Rex," Nancy said. "He can tell us how he got the blue off his hands when he was tricked."

Bess was careful not to touch anything as the girls left the trailer. Nancy took out her Clue Book. She stopped walking to cross the Fabuloso twins off her suspects list.

"We have no more suspects," Nancy said as she shut her book.

"Somebody in this circus switched my whistle!" George said. "We can't give up!"

As Nancy dropped her Clue Book in her pocket, she spotted a tall man with dark hair. It was Ringmaster Rex. He wasn't wearing his ring-master suit, but his twirly mustache twitched as he spoke on his phone. Rex didn't seem to see the girls as he turned away, still talking on the phone. . . .

"I told Mayor Strong that opening day was too important for a junior ringmaster!" Rex was saying in his usual booming voice.

The girls stopped in their tracks.

"Did he say junior ringmaster?" Nancy whispered.

"He's talking about me!" George hissed.

Nancy wanted to listen. She waved Bess and George behind a nearby tree. From there Ringmaster Rex's voice could be heard loud and clear.

"The junior ringmaster idea was a bad one," Rex went on, "but I'm glad I made the big switch!"

Nancy, Bess, and George exchanged wide-eyed stares. Did Ringmaster Rex say switch?

"The switch was worth it." Rex chuckled. "Who has the last laugh now? *This* guy!"

Ringmaster Rex ended the call. He pocketed his phone, and then he headed toward a nearby green-and-white trailer. Once he was inside, the girls darted out from behind the tree.

"Ringmaster Rex said he made a switch!" Bess said. "Could *he* have switched the whistles?"

"Rex said he didn't want a junior ringmaster," George said angrily. "He could have left me a broken whistle to make me look bad!"

"And just when we thought we had no more suspects," Nancy said, taking out her Clue Book. She wrote Ringmaster Rex's name on her suspect list.

"Let's go straight to Ringmaster Rex now!" George said, pointing to the trailer. "And demand to know where my whistle is!"

Nancy looked at Ringmaster Rex's trailer. Unlike George's, the windows were low.

"Let's peek through the window first," Nancy suggested. "Maybe we'll see the real whistle inside."

The girls scurried toward the trailer. When they peeked inside, the first thing they saw was Ringmaster Rex. He was standing in front of a mirror and peeling the mustache off his face!

"Omigosh!" Bess whispered. "Ringmaster Rex's famous mustache is fake!"

The girls watched as the ringmaster stuck his mustache on a piece of cardboard. The cardboard was lined with more twirly, swirly, and curly fake mustaches!

"Eenie, meenie, minie, mo," Ringmaster Rex said, pointing to each one. After choosing a big bushy mustache, he stuck it right on his face!

"Ringmaster Rex is tricking everybody with those fake mustaches!" George said, narrowing her eyes. "And I'll bet he tricked me by switching whistles!"

"We don't know for sure yet," Nancy said.

"I'm sure!" George said. "I want to knock on his door right now and—"

MWWWWAAAAAAAAAA!!!

The girls froze.

"What was that?" Nancy murmured.

Turning slowly, the girls gulped. Standing behind them was Shirley the Seesaw Llama. But this time she wasn't riding a seesaw with her owners.

This time she was *spitting*!

Chapter

ALL EARS

MWWWWAAAAAAAAAAA!!! Shirley groaned again.

Nancy, Bess, and George wanted to run, but Shirley was backing them against the trailer.

"Gob rockets!" George shouted as Shirley fired spit in the girls' direction. "Duck!"

The Clue Crew did a good job dodging Shirley's spit until Ringmaster Rex ran out of his trailer.

"What on earth is going on out here?" Rex demanded.

"Why don't you ask Shirley the Seesaw Llama?" George said. "She's the one who attacked us!"

The ringmaster looked at Shirley. His new mustache wiggled as he flashed a smile.

"You mean Shirley the *guard* llama," Rex replied.

"Guard llama?" Nancy repeated.

"Llamas are often used to guard sheep from coyotes," Rex explained. "Shirley was a guard llama before she joined the circus."

Ringmaster Rex reached out to gently pat Shirley. "I guess now she guards our trailers," he said.

When Shirley calmed down, Ringmaster Rex turned to George.

"Weren't you the junior ringmaster yesterday?" Rex asked. "The one with a whistling problem?"

"It wasn't George's fault, Ringmaster Rex," Nancy said. "Her whistle was switched with a broken one."

"We think the one who did the switcheroo," George said, folding her arms across her chest, "is you!"

"Me?" Ringmaster Rex exclaimed. "Why, I did nothing of the kind!"

"We overheard you talking on the phone," Nancy said. "You said something about making a switch."

"What else could it be but whistles?" Bess asked.

"How about . . . trailers?" Rex asked slowly.

"Trailers?" Nancy and her friends said together.

"Peggy asked me to switch trailers with the junior ringmaster," Rex explained. "My trailer was bigger and closer to the big tent."

"So why are you glad you made the switch?" Nancy asked.

"Because this one has Wi-Fi!" Rex said, pointing to the green-and-white trailer. "How cool is that?"

Ringmaster Rex tugged Shirley by her collar and said, "I'll bring Miss Shirley back to her owners now."

Nancy, Bess, and George watched as Ringmaster Rex gently led Shirley toward the tent.

"How do we know he told us the truth about switching trailers?" George asked.

"If Ringmaster Rex fooled us with his fake mustaches," Bess said, "he could be fooling us with a fake story!"

But the fake mustaches gave Nancy an idea.

"I know how we can find out if Ringmaster Rex is telling the truth," Nancy said. "We can give him an honesty test!"

The girls waited until the ringmaster returned.

"Ringmaster Rex?" Nancy asked bravely. "Is your mustache real . . . or fake?"

Ringmaster Rex's eyes widened. He glanced

both ways, and then he leaned over and whispered, "None of my mustaches are real. They're the press-on kind."

"No way!" Nancy said, pretending to be surprised.

"It's true," Rex admitted. "Now, can you girls promise to keep my mustaches a secret?"

"If you tell us another secret," Bess said. She raised her hands. "How do you get trick soap off?"

"Regular soap and water," Rex said with a grin. "Good luck!"

As the ringmaster walked into his trailer, Nancy crossed his name off her suspect list.

"If Ringmaster Rex was honest about his mustache," Nancy said, "he must be honest about switching trailers, not whistles."

"But now we have no suspects again." Bess frowned.

"What about Miles?" George said. "He didn't have to be a junior clown to be at the circus yesterday."

"How do we know Miles is really in Chicago,

filming a commercial for Super-Sour Suckers?" Bess said.

Nancy was about to give Miles a thought when—

"Girls?" someone called. "What are you still doing here?"

Nancy, Bess, and George whirled around. Walking toward them was the guard Fran.

"We were just leaving!" Nancy said.

"Did you find what you were looking for?" Fran asked.

Nancy thought about George's whistle and shook her head. "No," she replied, "but we're not going to give up!"

Bess didn't want to mess up Mr. Drew's car with her blue hands, so the Clue Crew walked back to Nancy's house. The girls all had the same rules: They could walk anywhere as long as it was fewer than five blocks away and they were together.

"We can work on our case while we eat lunch,"

Nancy said. "If we're lucky, Hannah will have lots of her yummy tuna salad."

"And real soap," Bess said, frowning down at her hands.

When the girls reached the Drew house, Bess went straight to the bathroom to wash her hands. Then they waited in Nancy's room while Hannah prepared lunch.

"I think I'll check my e-mails," George said as she sat at Nancy's computer and went online.

"Shouldn't we be working on the case?" Bess asked.

"We *are* working on the case," George said, staring at the computer screen. "I just got an e-mail from Miles!"

"Miles?" Nancy asked. She and Bess peered over George's shoulders as she read Miles's e-mail out loud: "'You may have won that dumb whistling contest, Fayne, but look what I'm getting to do. Jealous much?'"

Miles had attached a video. George clicked on it. The video showed Miles on a TV set!

"Super-Sour Suckers mean extreeeeme puckers!" Miles said into a camera. He popped a candy into his mouth. Soon his lips began to pucker—then his whole face!

"That's the same face Miles made at the whistle-blowing contest!" Bess said.

"Look!" Nancy said. She pointed to the date in the corner of the video. "That's the day George's whistle went missing."

"But how do we know he's filming the commercial in Chicago?" Bess asked.

"The cameraman is wearing a Cubs jersey," George pointed out. "That's a Chicago baseball team."

"So Miles wasn't around to switch whistles," Nancy decided, "instead he's a TV star."

"And I'm still a junior ringmaster with a busted whistle." George sighed. She pulled her broken whistle out and stuck it in her mouth.

"It's no use, George," Nancy said. "You're never going to get a sound out of that thing."

Woof! Woof! Woof!

Nancy's puppy, Chocolate Chip, suddenly came running in. George dropped the whistle as Chip jumped up on her, wagging her tail and still barking.

"You would think Chip heard my whistle!" George chuckled.

Nancy was about to call her dog, but then something suddenly clicked.

"You guys!" Nancy said. "Maybe Chip did!"

"Did what?" Bess asked.

Nancy smiled and said, "Maybe Chip did hear the whistle!"

Clue Crew—and YOU!

Can you solve the mystery of the circus whistle-switcher? Try thinking like the Clue Crew, or turn the page to find out!

1. The Clue Crew ruled out all their suspects. Can you think of others? Write them down on a piece of paper!

2. Nancy thinks that Chocolate Chip might have heard George's whistle. How would that be possible? Write down some reasons on a sheet of paper.

3. The Clue Crew discovered glitter and a red rubber clown nose in George's trailer. What other clues would you have looked for? Write your possible clues on a sheet of paper!

Chapter

BARK IN THE PARK

"I don't get it, Nancy," Bess said. "How could Chip hear the whistle when we didn't?"

"It might be a whistle that only dogs can hear," Nancy explained. "Dogs can hear things that humans can't."

"I've heard of dog whistles before!" George said. "Do you think this whistle is one?"

"Remember how Oodles of Poodles barked today at the circus?" Bess asked. "When you tried to blow your whistle, George?"

George nodded and said, "We didn't hear it, but the poodles did."

Nancy gave her puppy a big hug to say thanks. She had given them the best clue ever!

"I don't think the good whistle was switched with a broken whistle," Nancy said. "I think it was switched with a *dog* whistle!"

"But what if only Chip can hear it?" Bess asked. "We should test the whistle out on other dogs."

"Yes, and I know just the place to do it," Nancy said. "The dog run!"

Nancy, Bess, and George ate tuna sandwiches and then hurried to the dog run inside River Heights Park. From there they could see the circus tent.

"We've come to the right place," George said as they filed through the gate. "Look at all those dogs!"

Nancy saw dogs of all sizes,

scampering about with their owners. Would they stop playing if they heard the whistle? There was only one way to find out. . . .

"Okay, George," Nancy said. "Ready? Set? Blow!"

George stuck the whistle in her mouth and blew. Nancy didn't hear a thing, but that didn't matter. Could the dogs?

"Look!" Bess said, pointing to the dogs. One dropped his Frisbee as his ears perked up. Another was running toward George. Soon more dogs were charging toward George!

Woof, woof! Arf, arf!

"Testing complete!" George chuckled when she was surrounded by dogs. "My whistle *was* switched with a dog whistle!"

"There's only one dog act in the circus—Oodles of Poodles," Nancy said. "Maybe the whistle was Alberto's!"

"How do we know Alberto was in my trailer?" George asked. "The clown nose we found has nothing to do with dogs!"

Nancy watched as owners came to retrieve their dogs. One poodle reminded her of Alberto's dog, Celeste. That reminded her of something else. . . .

"Alberto's poodle wore a big collar just like a clown's," Nancy said. "Maybe part of her costume was a rubber clown *nose*!"

"Ewwww!" Bess exclaimed. "That means you tried on a dog's rubber nose, Nancy!"

Nancy didn't care. She just cared about putting the puzzle pieces together.

"I think the clown in George's trailer was funny and furry," Nancy declared. "I think the clown was a dog!"

The Clue Crew left the dog park and raced straight to the circus grounds. The show would start in a half-hour.

"How are we going to find Alberto?" Nancy asked.

"Here's how!" George said. She pulled out the whistle and blew. Soon—

Woof, woof, woof!

In a flash the Oodles of Poodles came running with Alberto right behind. The dogs were dressed up as clowns again. The only dog without a red rubber nose was Celeste!

"How did you get my dogs to run over?" Alberto asked.

"Easy!" George said, holding up the whistle. "Look familiar?"

Alberto's eyes popped open when he saw the whistle. He shook his head hard and stammered, "I—I—I don't remember!"

"Does this help your memory?" Nancy asked as she pulled the red rubber nose from her pocket.

When Alberto saw the nose, he gulped. He then took a deep breath and said, "That's my dog whistle. I left it in George's trailer."

Nancy's heart did a triple flip. Alberto had just confessed!

"The door was wide open," Alberto went on. "Celeste ran inside and under the table."

"But I closed the door when we left," George said.

"Maybe Fifi and Felix left the door open," Nancy figured, "when they left the trailer."

"I crawled under the table to get Celeste," Alberto continued, "but first I put my dog whistle on the table."

Alberto shrugged and said, "I grabbed Celeste, then my whistle before I left. I guess I grabbed the ringmaster whistle by mistake."

"And I got the dog whistle you left behind," George said glumly. "Thanks a lot, poodle boy."

"It was an accident!" Alberto said. "By the

time I knew I had the wrong whistle, you were already in the tent."

"Why didn't you tell us, Alberto?" Nancy asked.

"I felt too bad," Alberto admitted. "Because of me George's junior ringmaster moment was ruined."

Alberto reached into his pocket and pulled out a shiny silver whistle. It was so shiny that Nancy knew it was George's ringmaster whistle!

"Sorry," Alberto said as he handed the whistle to George.

Suddenly a frantic Peggy Bingle walked by.

"This is terrible!" Peggy was telling herself. "Simply terrible!"

"What's terrible, Ms. Bingle?" Nancy asked.

Peggy stopped and said, "The Fabuloso twins sprinkled itching powder in Ringmaster Rex's suit. He's refusing to do the show today!"

"Oh no!" Alberto said. "Who will blow the whistle to start the circus?"

George flashed a grin, and then she stuck the

shiny silver ringmaster whistle in her mouth. She puffed her cheeks and—

TWEEEEEEEEEEEEEEEEEEEEEEEEE!

"Oh my!" Peggy said, clapping both hands over her ears. Nancy and Bess smiled as they covered their ears too.

"Does that answer your question, Ms. Bingle?" George asked with a grin.

More circus people came out of their trailers to see what the noise was all about. Ringmaster Rex ran over too, itching and scratching all the way.

"Well, now," Rex told George, "I see you found your missing whistle."

"It's the real deal, Ringmaster Rex," Nancy said. "Now maybe you can give George another chance at being junior ringmaster."

"I can do better than that," Rex said with a grin. "George can be the *only* ringmaster in the show today!"

"Serious?" George gasped.

"Serious!" Rex replied. "Or . . . at least until I get a new suit."

"I have an idea too," Alberto said as he turned to Nancy and Bess. "How would you two like to be in the Oodles of Poodles act today?"

"Us?" Bess gasped.

"What would we do?" Nancy asked excitedly.

"You can hold the hoop while the dogs jump through," Alberto explained.

"Fun!" Bess cried happily.

"Oodles of fun!" Nancy exclaimed.

"Your ringmaster suit is still in your trailer, George," Peggy said. "I'll knock on your door when it's show time."

"Thanks, Ms. Bingle!" George said. "I know the drill!"

The circus people left to get ready for the show, and Nancy, Bess, and George high-fived. The Clue Crew had solved another case, but that wasn't all. . . .

"We're all going to be in the circus!" Nancy cheered. "How superamazingly cool is that?"

"I wonder what we're going to wear," Bess said excitedly.

"From now on I'm wearing my whistle around my neck!" George said. "After all, a good ringmaster never goes anywhere without her whistle."

"And a good detective," Nancy said with a smile, "never goes anywhere without her Clue Book!"

Test your detective skills with
even more Clue Book mysteries:

Nancy Drew Clue Book #5: Movie Madness

"How lucky are we to be living in Hollywood, you guys?" eight-year-old Bess Marvin asked excitedly.

Nancy Drew and George Fayne stopped walking to stare at Bess. Did she just say . . . Hollywood?

"Bess, we don't live in Hollywood," Nancy insisted. "We live in River Heights."

"Huge difference!" George pointed out.

"I know!" Bess agreed with a toss of her long

blond hair. "But a movie is about to be filmed right here. That makes River Heights practically Hollywood, right?"

"I guess!" Nancy said with a smile.

All three best friends had reason to smile: Summer vacation had just begun. Even better, a scene in the next Glam Girl action-adventure movie would be filmed right in their own neighborhood at Turtle Shell Playground!

"I still can't believe they're using kids from the neighborhood as movie extras!" Nancy said as they headed for the playground.

"Being in a movie will be cool," George admitted. "I just don't get why Glam Girl is so special."

"Are you serious, George?" Bess gasped. "Glam Girl is the only fashion-forward superhero who gets her powers from clothes!"

"A pair of sunglasses gives Glam Girl X-ray vision!" Nancy explained. "A hat lets her read minds, and gloves give her power to point and freeze any villain in his or her tracks!"

"Don't forget Glam Girl's electric-blue hair!" Bess said excitedly. "How awesome is that?"

"Sure, if you're a Smurf!" George snorted.

"Here's something awesome," Nancy added. "Shasta Sienna, the actress who plays Glam Girl, says she does all her own stunts—like jumping out of planes and off of speeding trains!"

"Stunts are cool," Bess said, "but I'm more interested in the clothes Glam Girl will wear in this movie."

George twisted one of her dark curls happily. "I'm interested in the special effects. Practically all movie special effects are computerized!"

"Computers, clothes—are you sure you're cousins?" Nancy asked Bess and George. "You're as different as—"

"River Heights and Hollywood!" George finished.

Bess was a serious fashionista with a room full of clothes and accessories. The only fashion accessory George dreamed of was a smartwatch!

"Speaking of movies," George said. "Look at who's up the block."

Nancy glanced ahead to see their classmate Sidney Schacter standing on his toes and taping a flier to a tree. Sidney was a major movie fanboy. He had even started his own movie-loving club called "Popcorn Peeps."

"Hi, Sidney," Nancy said as they walked over. "Are you going to be an extra in the Glam Girl movie today?"

"Nope," Sidney said. "I'd rather work on this!"

Sidney pointed proudly to the flier and said, "The Popcorn Peeps' first awesome movie museum in the basement of my house!"

New mystery. New suspense. New danger.

Nancy Drew DIARIES™

BY CAROLYN KEENE

EBOOK EDITIONS ALSO AVAILABLE   From Aladdin | simonandschuster.com/kids